CASTAWAYS!

Based on the TV series *Rugrats* created by Arlene Klasky, Gabor Csupo, and Paul Germain
and *The Wild Thornberrys* created by Klasky Csupo Inc., as seen on Nickelodeon.

POCKET
BOOKS

First published in Great Britain in 2003 by Pocket Books,
an imprint of Simon & Schuster UK Ltd
Africa House, 64-78 Kingsway, London WC2B 6AH

Originally published in 2003 by Simon Spotlight, an imprint of Simon & Schuster
Children's Publishing Division, New York.

POCKET BOOKS and colophon are registered trademarks of Simon & Schuster.
A CIP catalogue record for this book is available from the British Library

ISBN 0 743 47876 2

1 3 5 7 9 10 8 6 4 2

adapted by Sarah Willson

based on the screenplay by Kate Boutillier

illustrated by Patrick J. Dene, Bradley J. Gake, and Mike Giles

POCKET
BOOKS

Pocket Books/Nickelodeon

London   New York   Sydney

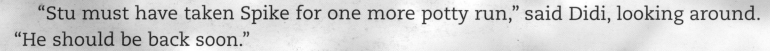

"Stu must have taken Spike for one more potty run," said Didi, looking around. "He should be back soon."

Everyone was eagerly waiting on the dock. They were all excited to board the world-famous *Lipschitz* cruise ship.

"He'd better come back soon," snapped Drew. "He has all our tickets!"

Tommy, Susie, and the other babies were waiting near the luggage.

"That sure is a nice cambera, Susie," said Tommy.

"Thanks," said Susie. "My mummy and daddy couldn't come along, so they gave it to me to take pictures to show them."

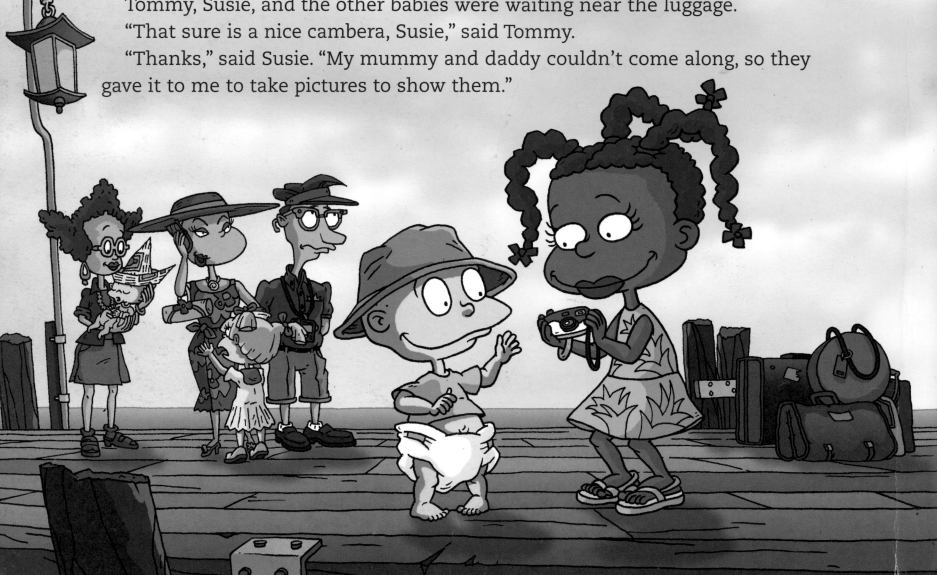

All of a sudden Howard let out an alarmed cry.
"Hey!" he said. "Is it me, or is the dock moving?"
"The ship is sailing without us!" yelled Drew.

Toot-toot! Everyone turned from the departing ship to see a tiny boat chugging towards them. Stu was at the helm.

"Ahoy, mates!" he called heartily. "Climb aboard for seven fun-filled days on the SS *Nancy*. No fancy packaged tour – just the thrill of the open sea, the smell of the salt air, and the joy of close friends and family!"

The grown-ups gaped at the tiny boat in disbelief.

"I can't believe you did this!" said Chas angrily.

"We'll follow the *Lipschitz* cruise ship and board it at the first port," declared Drew.

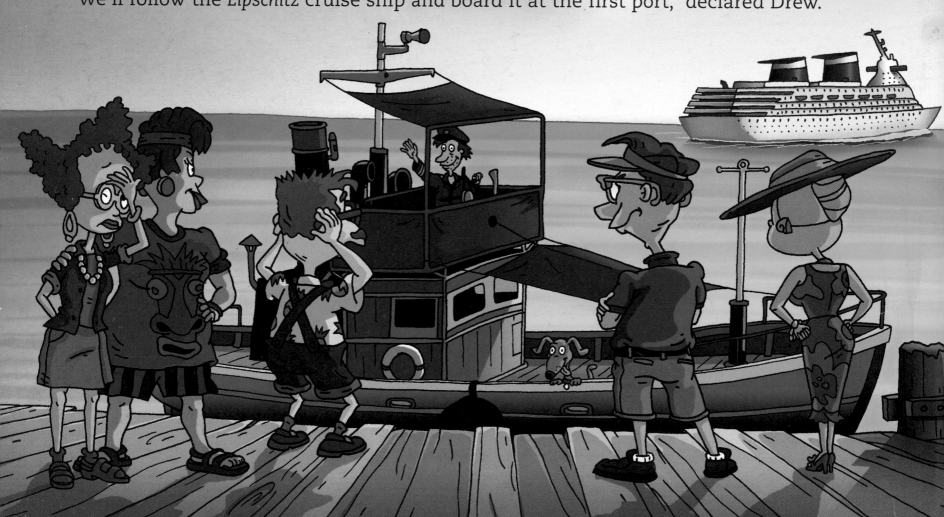

No sooner had they set sail than the skies opened.
Rain poured down. Thunder boomed. Lightning flashed.
"Everyone get below!" yelled Betty.

A wave crashed over the tiny boat, sending it up into
the air. It landed upside down in the churning waters.
Below deck everything turned topsy-turvy.

Water began pouring in. "Abandon ship!" yelled Stu. "Grab the kids and get out!" They all bobbed to the surface. "The boat is sinking!" yelled Charlotte.

Suddenly Betty's head and shoulders burst out of the water. "I took a minute to grab a few things I thought might come in handy," she said, grinning. She held up Dil's dummy and folded-up stroller. Then she pulled on a cord attached to a yellow square under her arm. An inflatable lifeboat sprang open. Everyone jumped in.

The storm passed. Night fell and everyone drifted off to sleep.

Early the next morning the lifeboat jolted to a stop. Everyone woke up.

"Land ho!" said Stu. They had washed up on a sandy beach. The babies and their parents stepped out of the lifeboat. "I know exactly where we are! See? We're on this tiny little island called . . . Uninhabited," said Stu, studying his soggy map.

"Drew!" yelled Charlotte. "The lifeboat is gone!"

"You didn't tie up the lifeboat?" Drew angrily asked Stu.

"I meant to . . . " said Stu. The lifeboat drifted out to sea.

"We're stranded! With no food!" moaned Howard.

"We need some order here!" barked Betty. "Stu, you keep an eye on the kids. The rest of you, follow me."

The adults built a playpen for the babies. Inside, Tommy had an idea.

"Look! I think it's the topical drain forest – just like we sawed on Nigel Strawberry's telabision show!"

Nigel Thornberry was one of Tommy's heroes.

"I bet if we go in there, we'll find him," said Tommy. "Nigel Strawberry knows all about the great outbores. He can help us get home! Who wants to help me look for him?"

"We all will!" said Susie.

"Not me," said Angelica. "You babies won't last a second in that drain forest!"

But Susie and the babies were already heading towards the forest.

While the other grown-ups followed Betty's orders, Stu began collecting things on the beach. Angelica marched over to him.

"What's all this junk, Uncle Stu?" asked Angelica.

"It's not junk," he replied. "These everyday items can be used to make lots of things . . . like a radio. That's it – I'll build a radio and send a distress signal! Angelica, keep an eye on the babies for a minute, okay?" He hurried away.

"But they went off into the drain forest!" scoffed Angelica. "Spike! Wake up and go and get the babies."

Tommy and the babies walked through the dark rain forest. Soon Chuckie needed a break.
"I think I need to find a potty," he said, walking towards the trees.
When Chuckie emerged, the others were nowhere to be seen. "Guys? Wait up!" he called.
As Chuckie was looking for the others, he tripped and dove headlong into a muddy puddle.
Chuckie tottered over to a stream to wash the mud off. As he took off his clothes and his glasses he heard a strange sound.

Somebody crept over to Chuckie's clothes and swiped his shorts and shirt. In their place a different pair of shorts appeared. Chuckie felt around blindly and found the shorts, which he put on. "What happened to my shoes and my glasses?" he asked out loud.

A wild-looking boy, who looked a lot like Chuckie, quickly put on Chuckie's clothes, shoes, and glasses. The boy's name was Donnie. He scampered away into the woods.

Chuckie groped his way farther into the forest, in the opposite direction.

Tommy and the other babies were about to go and look for Chuckie, when Donnie appeared – in Chuckie's clothing. Donnie jabbered something.

"Uh, are you okay, Chuckie?" asked Tommy.

Donnie motioned for them to follow, and then bounded away.

"Hey, since when did Chuckie start talking backwards?" asked Phil.

Meanwhile Nigel Thornberry was searching nearby for the never-before-photographed clouded leopard. Suddenly at the bottom of the cliff, Donnie appeared with Tommy and the babies. Nigel picked up his binoculars.

"Mr Strawberry!" yelled Susie.

"What are these babies doing here?" Nigel exclaimed. "Stay there, children! I'm coming down!"

As Nigel started down the cliff he fell and hit his head. He got up, dazed.

"Are you okay, Mr Strawberry?" asked Susie.

"Why are you calling me 'mister'?" asked Nigel. "I'm only this many years old," he said, extending three fingers. "Do any of you remember where I left my tricycle?"

"Uh, no, Mr Strawberry," replied Susie. "We're shipwrecked on this island. We was hoping you could help Tommy's daddy."

"Look what I can do!" Nigel shouted, standing on his head. "Oopsie-daisy!"

"Tommy, I think Nigel Strawberry is acting kind of funny," said Susie.

"Maybe he's got diapie rash," said Lil.

Not far away Tommy's dog, Spike, was sniffing around, searching frantically for the missing babies. Spike nearly stumbled over a girl who sat listening to the chattering of a chimp. The girl and the chimp both looked up at Spike in surprise.

"Uh, hi!" said the girl to Spike. "I'm Eliza Thornberry." Eliza could talk to animals. "Are you looking for something?"

"Yeah," said Spike. "I'm looking for my babies, but I can't find them anywhere."

"Don't worry," said Eliza. "We'll help you look for them."

Suddenly a leopard sprang in front of them.
"Oh, my!" exclaimed Eliza. "You're a . . ."
"I'm Siri, the clouded leopard," said Siri.
"I'm Spike, the purebred mutt!" joked Spike.
"Look at my claws," hissed Siri.
Darwin screamed.

"I'm going to miss our island," said Chas.
Didi proposed a toast. "To the best holiday we ever had!"
"To Stu!" said everyone.

The babies, meanwhile, ate cookies and drank juice.

"Well, guys. We did it!" said Tommy. "We found Nigel Strawberry and no one's mad anymores."

"Pickles, you may grow up to be just like Nigel Strawberry after all," said Angelica.

"Thanks, Angelica," said Tommy. "But I think I'll grow up to be just like my daddy."